D0027840

# Blue's Clues

# My Dress-up Party

by Sarah Willson
illustrated by Jennifer Oxley

Ready-to-Read

Simon Spotlight/Nick Jr.

New York    London    Toronto    Sydney    Singapore

Based on the TV series *Blue's Clues*® created by Traci Paige Johnson,
Todd Kessler, and Angela C. Santomero as seen on Nick Jr.®
On *Blue's Clues,* Joe is played by Donovan Patton. Photos by Joan Marcus.

SIMON SPOTLIGHT
An imprint of Simon & Schuster Children's Publishing Division
1230 Avenue of the Americas, New York, New York 10020
Copyright © 2003 Viacom International Inc. All rights reserved.
NICKELODEON, NICK JR., *Blue's Clues,* and all related titles, logos, and characters are
trademarks of Viacom International Inc.
READY-TO-READ, SIMON SPOTLIGHT and colophon are registered trademarks of
Simon & Schuster.
Manufactured in the United States of America
First Edition
2 4 6 8 10 9 7 5 3 1

Library of Congress Cataloging-in-Publication Data

Willson, Sarah.
My dress-up party / by Sarah Willson.—1st ed.
p. cm.—(Ready-to-read ; #6)
Summary: Blue has a dress-up party but only finds a costume for herself
at the last minute.
ISBN: 0-689-85229-0
[1. Costume — Fiction. 2. Parties — Fiction.]
I. Oxley, Jennifer - ill. II. Title. III. Series.
PZ7.W6845My 2003
[E] 21                                                                    2002006030

Hi! I am 🐾 . We are
BLUE
having a dress-up
party! Joe is hanging
🎈 all over the 🏠 .
BALLOONS                    HOUSE

Mr. Salt and
Mrs. Pepper baked
a ![cake] CAKE .

Paprika will scoop out the . Yum!

ICE CREAM

Now we can set the  with

TABLE

,  ,

PLATES

FORKS

and ‼ !

SPOONS

It is time to dress up!
Tickety Tock is going
as a grandfather CLOCK.

# Mailbox is wearing a  costume.

MAILMAN

# Mr. Salt and Mrs. Pepper are dressed up as .

CHEFS

# Paprika is going as a .

SPOON

Joe and I still need costumes. We can look in Joe's 🧺 .

CLOSET

Maybe his  will
give us an idea.

SHOES

He can be a
BASEBALL
player, an ice-skater,
or pretend he is
going to the .
BEACH

Look at all the

HATS

in my 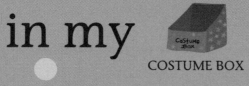 .

COSTUME BOX

I could be an ,

ASTRONAUT

a , or a .

FIREFIGHTER        FARMER

# The guests are already at the ⌂ !

DOOR

Magenta came as

a .

Periwinkle is wearing

a 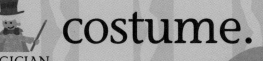 costume.

We still need costumes!
What else is in
my  ?

COSTUME BOX

I think Joe has an idea. What could he do with these ⋀⋀ ?

SOCKS

# Now I am dressed like .

JOE

And Joe is dressed
like me, !

BLUE

It is time for ICE CREAM and 🍰 . Thank you for coming!

CAKE